This book belongs to

....

This edition published by Parragon Books Ltd in 2017

Parragon Books Ltd
Chartist House
15–17 Trim Street
Bath BA1 1HA, UK
www.parragon.com

Illustrated by: Gavin Scott
Reading consultant: Geraldine Taylor

ISBN 978-1-4748-9519-4

Printed in China

My First Storytime
Goldilocks
and the
Three Bears

PaRRagon

Bath • New York • Cologne • Melbourne • Delhi
Hong Kong • Shenzhen • Singapore

Five steps for enjoyable reading

Traditional stories and fairy tales are a great way to begin reading practice. The stories and characters are familiar and lively. Follow the steps below to help your child become a confident and independent reader:

One day, Goldilocks was walking in the woods. Yum! She could smell something tasty. It was coming from the little house.

8

Step 1
Read the story aloud to your child. Run your finger under the words as you read.

Step 2
Look at the pictures and talk about what is happening.

Step 3

Read the simple text on the right-hand page together. When reading, some words come up again and again, such as **the, to, and**. Your child will quickly get to recognize these high-frequency words by sight.

Who lives here?" said Goldilocks.

9

Step 4

When your child is ready, encourage them to read the simple lines on their own.

Step 5

Help your child to complete the puzzles at the back of the book.

One day, Goldilocks was walking in the woods. Yum! She could smell something tasty. It was coming from the little house.

"Who lives here?" said Goldilocks.

9

Goldilocks knocked on the door.
But there was no reply. Goldilocks pushed
the door. It swung open, but there was no
one there. Goldilocks stepped inside!

There were three bowls of hot
porridge on the table.

The tasty smell was making
Goldilocks feel hungry!
She tasted the big
bowl of porridge.
It was too salty.

Next, she tasted
the middle-sized
bowl of porridge.
It was too sweet.

Finally, she tasted the little bowl
of porridge...

It was just right! Goldilocks ate it all up.

Goldilocks needed to sit
down after all that
yummy porridge.
She sat on the
big chair. It
was too high.

She sat on the
middle-sized chair.
It was too low.

She sat on the little chair...

Oh no! Goldilocks broke the little chair!

Goldilocks crept upstairs. There were
three beds. She tried the big bed. It was
too hard.

She tried the middle-sized bed.
It was too soft.

She tried the little bed...

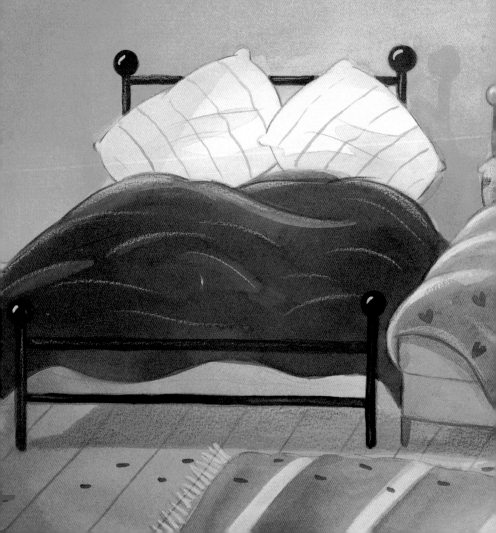

It was just right! Goldilocks took a nap.

But while Goldilocks was asleep, three
hungry bears came back to the house.
They were looking forward to eating
their porridge!

The three bears looked at their bowls
of porridge.

"Who's been eating my porridge?"
roared Daddy Bear.

"Who's been eating my porridge?"
growled Mummy Bear.

"Who's eaten my porridge ALL UP?"
squeaked Baby Bear.

"What will I eat?" cried Baby Bear.
He was sad.

"Who's been sitting in my chair?"
roared Daddy Bear.

"Who's been sitting in my chair?"
growled Mummy Bear.

"Who's been sitting in
my chair and BROKEN IT?"
squeaked Baby Bear.

"Where will I sit?" said Baby Bear.

"Who's been sleeping in my bed?"
roared Daddy Bear.

"Who's been sleeping in my bed?"
growled Mummy Bear.

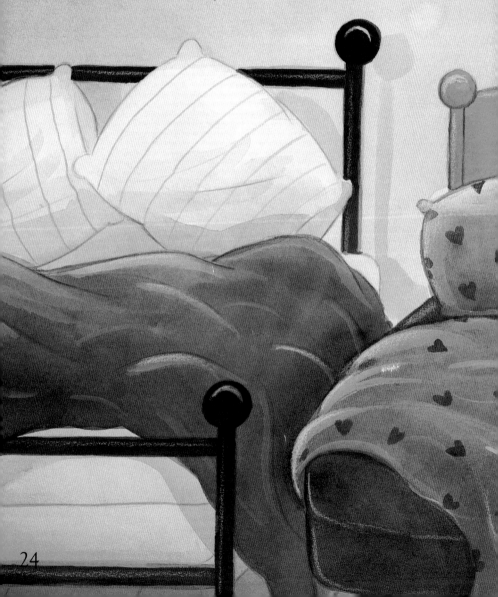

"Who is in my bed?"
said Baby Bear.

Suddenly, Goldilocks woke up and saw three bears! She jumped up and ran away. And the three bears never saw her again!

She ran as fast as she could all the
way home.

Puzzle time!

Which two words rhyme?

sit sad not run hot

Which word does not match the picture?

bowl

porridge

chair

Which word matches the picture?

bear

wear

pear

Who breaks the chair?

Goldilocks

Daddy Bear

Baby Bear

Which sentence is right?

This bed was just right.

This bed was not right.